NO WAY OUT

Santana Knox

Editor: Alexa @ The Fiction Fix

Cover design: Leah Maree – Design by LM

Internal art: Brianna Billiard, @Flashfryed

Contents

Content Warnings

Ohio, gruesome murders, strangling, disembowelment, blood-play, dubcon, noncon, unprotected sex, masked sexual encounters, hay, coercion, blackmail, lukewarm necrophilia, stabbing, sexual assault, maiming, bootlicking, light fisting, arson, impact play, DP, DVP, stretching.

From the author:

This story is a horror romance/Erotic horror. It features relationship dynamics that are not only unhealthy but criminal. As always, I have to remind my readers that these stories are just the intrusive thoughts that live in the dark corners of my mind. Please take your mental health seriously and do not continue to read if you find any of the elements in this book too disturbing.

With that being said, welcome to No Way Out.

If you know me in real life, no you don't.

To Ohio. You fucked me up good

You are the altar, not the sacrifice.

ONE
DON'T MIX CLIQUES

"I heard he got caught finger-blasting Jolie Parker in the bleachers during the pep rally rehearsal." I could hear Delaney Summers talking about my personal life as if she didn't see me walking three feet in front of her.

I buried my face in my hands and groaned. It had only been fifteen hours since I was publicly dumped by the captain of the football team in front of his entire fraternity. By breakfast, the entire student body had heard the news; someone even went viral for sharing the video.

I had no business getting involved with him. I was black cargo pants and twelve year old converse shoes being held together solely by good vibes and wishful thinking, and he was pastel polo shirts and Adidas with pristine white socks, the kind of shoes that never looked stained or dingy because someone paid to replace them before they ever got bad.

Aside from the embarrassment of having the entire Kappa Sigma witnessing my breakup, I was mostly relieved—ecstatic, even, that I wouldn't have to do another year of pretending to give a rat's ass about entitled rich boys who couldn't even clean their own rooms. I thought Noah was different, but clearly, I was wrong. I was thrilled that I was no longer going to be dragged to every sporting event and forced to smile at every sexual harassment lawsuit in waiting. Relief aside, that didn't mean I was stoked to hear my boyfriend of three years was already moving on.

We had met during freshman orientation, and in a way, we sort of grew up together.

I didn't really think we'd make it out of college, buy an apartment together, get married, have kids. We were far too different, and as time went on, our interests grew further and further apart. I was a vegan, and he still couldn't comprehend why I wouldn't just want to 'pick the meat off' my food.

My heart wasn't shattered; I just cared about being humiliated.

Stupid pride.

"Oops; sorry, Camila," Delaney giggled from behind me to her crew of petty bitches in cheerleading uniforms. "Didn't see you there, babe," she mocked before walking past me, tossing her hand through my hair to dishevel it.

I fumed internally, but the only sign of my emotions was my flared nostrils, and the only person who could see them right now was my best friend, Naya.

"Fuck her. It's probably not even true." She popped her gum casually as we made our way to Botanical sciences.

The leaves crunched beneath our feet as we walked, the weather already requiring multiple layers.

Standard Ohio October bullshit.

The screeching of a motorcycle coming to a halt in front of the Natural Sciences building was almost as loud as the gasping of the Kappa Hoe-ntourage in matching pink tennis skirts in front of us. Intrusive thoughts of punching through Delaney Summer's orbital socket flashed through my head, I squeezed my fist on instinct, as if her eyeball would somehow manifest between my fingers.

Heavy leather boots crushed piles of dead leaves, turning them into powdered versions of themselves as a black-cladded knight dismounted his Ducati. I knew its purr well, and from the sound alone, I could have guessed the speedbike was at least an 800. I licked my lips at the sight of the sunlight reflecting off the chrome, but I looked away just in time before its owner could catch me.

Helmet still covering his face, he stalked past me, the scent of citrus and leather whipping through my senses, the hairs on my arm standing up in alarm. Naya gave me a look full of dark suggestions only my best friend could think up in such a small amount of time, but I shook my head at her and followed him from a distance as we walked into the building.

Focusing on my thesis was the only thing I cared about right now. If I worked my ass off, there was a good chance I could graduate before fall semester ended, and then I wouldn't ever have to deal with Noah or any of these fucking assholes ever again.

"But you *are* still coming to the homecoming corn maze thing, aren't you?" Naya was already whining, like she knew I was going to find any reason possible to back out of a public event.

Naya and I had been pals since grade school, neighbors who grew up together on the same street. We became fast friends when we realized we both had five siblings. Our perfect match was confirmed with a dual obsession for the strange and unusual. After high school, we both applied to NPC for undergrad, and now that we were almost done, we would surely make plans to stay close.

Co-dependent was our vibe.

"Kyle Danvers asked to pick me up." She grinned, and I delayed my reaction. "For the corn maze. Camila, are you even listening to me?" She huffed, not shying away from displaying her annoyance. "It's that dumb twat, isn't it?" She turned around, baring her teeth at the cheerleaders.

They gasped, freezing in place and allowing more distance to grow between us.

I was anxious, and rightfully so. Noah and I had been blurring the lines between cliques for three years, and now that our relationship was over, all the repressed dislike and forced smiles were sure to come flooding out like a broken dam. Exhibit A: the group of cheerleaders following behind me like a pack of hyenas who smelled an injured gazelle.

I crossed the threshold into the plant sciences wing, and the vultures behind me stopped circling, choosing instead to march on, straight to wherever they were needed most. I laughed at the thought of them even being needed somewhere.

"I'm not going." I stood my ground as we placed our books down onto our table.

"Mila, don't be a pain in the ass. Who's gonna make sure I get home safely without any roofies?" She nudged me.

"Bitch, you'd take the roofies yourself if someone offered," I snarked, and we broke out in a loud laugh just as Dr. Harkins walked into the lab.

He raised an eyebrow. "Something funny, Miss Machado?" The corner of his lip tugged upward, but he had too much control over it to let any of us see.

Demetri Harkins was drool-worthy. I'd been studying under him for the last two years, ever since he and his doctoral degree in plant biology appeared at NPC out of nowhere and demanded to be fit into the curriculum. I changed my major from Biology to Botany the minute it became available.

It wasn't because of his dark hair that sat perfectly groomed on top of his head, aside from the little wave that swooped down just above his eyes. It certainly wasn't because of his bright green eyes or the tattoo of the Death Star that peeked out from his rolled-up shirt on the inside of his elbow. It *definitely* had nothing to do with the way the sleeves perfectly squeezed his muscled biceps when he rolled them up every morning when he got to class.

No, those were just perks.

I'd been obsessed with plants my whole life. I learned basic herbology from my Macumbeira grandmother before I turned ten. By seventeen, I had written a book on how to kill someone and get away with it using only plants. The Nile publishing services still banned it after a week—something about its "dangerous potential".

I don't know—sometimes, a girl needs to know how to off a man in an untraceable way. I still didn't see the issue there.

"N-No. Nothing funny, Dr. Harkins," I managed to rush out of my mouth.

"Just discussing the highly severe implications drug addiction can have." Naya barely held it together, her laugh hissing out like a gas leak between words.

"Save it for a relevant class, girls." Before he could move on, the start of class was once again interrupted, this time by a student pausing at the door.

Remaining in Harkins' good graces was necessary if I were to graduate a semester early. Hopefully, if I did, he'd sign a referral for my employment as the herbology specialist on campus. A job straight out of college was practically unheard of these days.

I couldn't fuck that up.

NPC was a pretty big campus, but not large enough that I didn't recognize most of the people in my program, and this guy was *not* in it. He was at least six foot five from the way he towered over Dr. Harkins. Naya and I had pretty much visually measured our professor for the last two years, and we felt confident in our conclusion that he was between six and six feet two inches tall. With his helmet held tightly against his side, mystery-man raked his fingers through his shiny black hair before approaching Harkins' desk.

"Can I help you?" my annoyed professor asked.

He stayed silent, handing over a piece of paper to the professor, not turning his head to the rest of the class. I could only see about half of his face, and the half I could see was covered by hair, multiple lip piercings, and what looked to be a tattoo of a rose gracing his neck.

A black, button-down shirt and matching checkered vans were apparently enough to do it for me; suddenly, I was no longer questioning my fuck face ex's ability to move on so fast.

"Did you find a new toy to ride?" Naya whispered in my ear, as if she could hear my lady juice dripping down to my underwear.

"You have no self control." I shook my head, clamping my lips together to hold back my smile as our professor quietly spoke to what looked to be a new student.

It was October—it was way too fucking late to be joining the semester.

"Miss Costa, please join another lab duo for the semester and clear out the seat next to Miss Machado for our new student," Dr. Harkins announced.

We groaned simultaneously.

"Any duo," he reminded her, and my bestie's loyalty evaporated, her eyes going wide as she scrambled to pick up her books and join Kyle Danvers' lab group.

Asshole. I communicated with her telepathically, pretending like she'd receive the message.

It would make me feel better.

Then, I turned my head, my attention focused on the black hole circling toward me.

I swallowed the hard lump in my throat.

"Camila, Zeke is a late transfer from West Haven Parochial. His focus is on herbology and plant energy just like you. I'd like you to help him catch up, please."

I nodded, my mouth slightly agape as I watched one of the most attractive men I'd ever seen in my life move toward me like a gift from the gods.

TWO
FUCKING OHIO

"I can't believe I'm going to this stupid fucking corn maze." Naya's eyes went wide, as if my mood offended her. "Sorry, I didn't mean to say that out loud," I lied, taking advantage of the fact that she understood how difficult it was to hold on to those intrusive thoughts sometimes.

"Sure." She rolled her eyes, grabbing my wrist and pulling me from the parking lot before I had a chance to even lock my car.

Rural Ohio.

Yup.

The corn maze was a joke of a holiday event, because regardless of whether it was Halloween, it would probably still exist. This entire *state* was a fucking corn maze, plus Cedar Point.

Corn mazes and Cedar Point. The only good thing about this place was that when winter came, you could leave your beer outside to keep it cold.

"I swear to all that is dark and unholy, if you leave me for the Danvers kid tonight, you will feel my wrath," I said in my most emotionless tone possible.

"I love when you get all hexen-witch on me," she giggled, hooking her arm into mine as we walked toward the ticket booth.

It felt like the whole town was here tonight. Granted, Hiram was tiny enough as it was, but cramming the whole town into a couple of acres of corn was a wild idea. I felt a cool breeze against my neck, and my flesh exploded in goosebumps. I should have brought a jacket. This time of year was already cold, usually teasing the idea of snow by Halloween. This morning had been so hot, I didn't even think to grab anything for when the sun set; by night, I would regret my decision.

It would be a good excuse to leave earlier than planned without Naya giving me hell.

The line to get through the gates was long as hell, the screaming of happily frightened children polluting the air. Their parents blissfully ignored the sounds as they contentedly sipped their overpriced beers and concession stand hot chocolates.

Colored lights hung on strings from tent to tent. There was a fun house attraction, red and white tented roofs with a poorly painted sign that read 'Carnival' with a missing letter 'I'. The line for the hayride, though, was the longest. In the distance, the leaf blowers could be heard, mimicking chainsaws as the scare actors moved from person to person, hoping to get a fearful reaction.

"Didn't think you'd be the type to show up to this kind of thing, Miss Machado." The sound of my professor's gravely voice came directly from behind me, the mint of his gum so cool, I swear I could feel it on my neck with the brush of the wind. The scent of something woodsy, like the spiced cedar of his cologne I knew well, invaded my senses.

My skin pebbled, and I exhaled, still not daring to turn around and face the handsome teacher only six years my senior. Seeing Demetri Harkins outside of the college grounds was dangerous. Every interaction we'd had without other students around felt too tense, unbearably heavy with the electricity of our undeniable attraction.

Well, undeniable to *me*.

"I-I was forced," I stuttered before spinning to face him.

He grinned. That damn smile.

Shit.

It was even better out in the real world than it was in class.

Stupid, dimpled, gorgeous, perfectly straight teeth with sharp canines that should be forbidden on hot professors.

"I'm happy to take any students held against their will back to their dorms," he said with a straight face.

Naya was still facing forward, but the squeal that came from her was loud enough to paint my entire face red.

"I appreciate the offer. I'll let you know if I'm under duress. Alas, I'm here, so I might as well suffer through some... research. Of the vegetation, of course." The words fumbled out of my mouth faster than my brain could process them.

Naya laughed, and Harkins bit his cheek, as if to hold back the corner of his lip from curling further.

"Of course. It's good to do social things sometimes, even if the company isn't the most agreeable," he said, as if two years of exposure to my mind was enough to hack into my brain.

He knew my threshold for people was a maximum of two or three at a time.

He pointed forward to let us know it was our turn to buy tickets.

I blacked out.

My heart was beating so fast from the interaction, I couldn't remember pulling my wallet out or even speaking to the booth attendant. I felt the pressure of my best friend's palm on my back and the muddled echo of her voice trying to reach me, and suddenly, I found us sitting on a nearby bench just past the gates.

I waited for some sort of clarity to return to me. Dr. Harkins was nowhere in sight—not that my vision was reliable at the moment. It was tunneled and foggy, partly from adrenaline, but mostly from embarrassment and desire. "I told you he was gonna wait until graduation to fuck you," Naya said, as if she'd already been planning the whole thing.

I breathed in and out through my nose a few more times before I could actually generate words from my throat.

"Okay, but that was direct as hell, right? Or did I read too much into it?" I asked, starting to wonder if maybe I was over-thinking it and fabricating my own version of the event.

"You think too much. He fucking wants you. *Camila Harkins.*" She sighed, falling onto my lap dramatically.

"Idiot." I rolled my eyes. "I feel better now—panic attack averted. Let's fucking do this and get out of here."

"You know this is an event, right? Not a chore to get through. It's *supposed* to be fun." She pointed her fingers to her mouth and faked a giant smile.

"Why would hundreds of people gathering in a small loca-tion, with very little way to get out in case of an emergency, sound like fun? Oh, and there's *children*, too." I wrinkled my nose at the little shitling running by with sticky fingers and a runny nose.

I'd be sick by Wednesday.

For sure.

I stood up, brushing some stray hay from my clothes as we made our way to the corn maze.

"Okay, but can we circle back to Harkins' class today? That new guy was hot as shit! Did you see those lip rings? I love a pierced guy. That almost always means they're pierced down below, too." She raised her eyebrows and licked her lips at the same time.

"You're impossible." I hit her with the back of my hand, and she faked injury, opening her mouth widely in shock as she went full drama. "I'd ride his face though." I grinned, giving my best friend exactly what she wanted.

THREE
SCARECROW

I'd watched her throughout the entirety of class, averting my eyes and pretending to stare somewhere else anytime the heat of her gaze caught me. It was difficult to pretend not to be interested, to act like she wasn't the most beautiful person in the room.

Yet here she was again, within my reach, as if neither one of us could bear to stay away. She was a magnet, and I was the metal, drawn to her by the sheer command of science.

I'd been forced into this stupid costume. The scarecrow mask resembled more like the one from *The Dark Knight* than it did the things perched out in the fields. I slipped it over my head as I made my way to the center of the maze, making sure to keep track of which right turns I took and counting one, two, three, lefts before every right. It was the only way to find the center, and there was only one way out from there.

They'd paid some super genius fifteen year old who was getting his masters in coding to calculate the hardest possible maze, charging over a hundred bucks per ticket in the name of fundraising. The first person out of the maze would win five hundred dollars.

Not bad, but they were hoping no one would make it out in the end. At any point, they could call for help, admit defeat, and be escorted out by any of the scare volunteers. There's a good amount of us hiding in the field, in the wall of corn that blocks anything from view. I heard Naya Costa's scream in the distance, knowing it wouldn't be long until I got my first chance to encounter the raven-haired girl I couldn't erase from my head.

I climbed onto the post, taking my place up high where I could see a large portion of the labyrinth, and prepared for the night, unsure of what would happen once I made my move.

If she didn't want me...

I didn't know what I would do.

Camila Machado wasn't from this world. She couldn't be. She was soft but sharp, dark with madness but filled with a radiant light. Her obsidian-black hair reflected blue in the moonlight, those dark, hooded eyes slathered in charcoal-like makeup with little care, smudging in the corners and somehow making her look even more radiant.

She was wearing a black mesh shirt, buttoned all the way up to the collar, with nothing but a matching bra underneath. A dark gray and black pleated skirt barely covered her ass, and matching striped socks stopped at her knees. She finished the look with leather boots; perfection.

With a sigh, I stilled my body, doing my best to contribute to the illusion that I was a mere prop for the visitors' Halloween experience.

FOUR
WITH FRIENDS LIKE THESE

"Why do you keep looking around?" I finally asked her.

"What do you mean?" Naya played dumb, like she didn't understand what I was asking.

That made her look even guiltier.

"Bitch, you literally keep looking over your shoulders every five seconds like a goddamn cokehead in debt." I set my hands on my hips as she gave me a weird smile that reeked of guilt. "You fucking didn't." My jaw went slack in disbelief of her audacity.

"I mean, how could I not? Don't be mad!" she whined, hugging onto me.

Just as I pushed her off I heard him approaching from behind.

"Hey, mama." Kyle Danvers tried his best husky voice on her, and I bit back a laugh at him trying to sound like he had any sort of charm at all.

He dropped his arm around her shoulder and pulled her in for a kiss. I peeled my upper lip up but immediately corrected, feigning niceness for the sake of my best friend.

I knew Kyle, and his type was just another flavor of my ex, Noah Corinth. They were all exactly the same, printed in the same factory and shipped out in the same batch. Kyle Danvers was there, cheering Noah on while cheerleader after cheerleader stood in line to suck his best friend's dick. I was forced to hold in my tears last night, forced to pretend like the last three years had meant nothing to me while his fraternity brothers blocked me from leaving the room, trapping me and giving me no choice but to listen, my eyes drifting anywhere they could to avoid watching my ex getting his cock deepthroated just inches away.

The lesson apparently *wasn't* for me; I was just collateral damage.

Kappas don't dwell on the past, and the only way to prove it to his brothers was to humiliate me.

Kyle Danvers thought fucking with girls like us was nothing but a joke, something to pass the time until the next entertaining thing happened. For three years, he treated me like a punchline waiting to drop, and when it finally happened, he couldn't wait to laugh in my face.

"Is it cool if we kick it with you ladies?" Kyle handed Naya a red plastic cup filled with beer, and his buddy tried handing me another.

"No, thanks." I waved it off, shrugging at Kyle's request, knowing damn well I was going to come off like a bitter asshole if I said no to them hanging out with us.

"You don't drink?" His friend asked. I'd seen him before, but he must have been a year or two younger, because I couldn't for the life of me remember seeing him in any classes.

"I don't like how it makes me feel. If you have weed, though, I'll smoke the shit out of it," I told him.

He shook his head, and the line to enter the maze moved, getting us closer to our turn.

"This is taking forever." Naya exaggerated *forever* like she was putting on a show for Kyle.

I glanced at her cup, seeing that it was almost empty.

Kyle caught my gaze, but he was on an entirely different wavelength. "I'll go grab you another." He kissed her cheek and walked away, his buddy following right by his side.

"Thank you," she whispered.

I rolled my eyes again. "I will hit him in the mouth if he even mentions last night," I warned her.

"That's totally fair. I'll text him a heads up." She nodded eagerly like I'd finally given her permission to have fun.

I knew I was being a sour bitch, but I definitely felt like it was in my right to commit some wrongs for at least the next week.

The universe owed it to me.

I felt the heat of someone's stare on me, but I couldn't pinpoint who. I hated being out in the open like this, exposed like krill waiting for the whale to open its mouth and devour me.

They would cease to exist before they could realize they were dead.

Maybe it was a blessing.

"Hey, isn't that the new guy?" Naya nudged me with her shoulder, using her head to point toward the black haired, lanky, broody guy who'd dropped into my almost-literal lap today. "What was his name?"

"Zeke, Ezekiel, something like that." I feigned disinterest, knowing she would lose it if I mentioned how good he smelled, or how deep and low his voice sounded in my ear when he asked me a question.

She would make far too much of a deal about it.

"I bet those lip rings would feel so goo-" She moaned just as Kyle cleared his throat, announcing his untimely return.

"What would feel good?" he said with a smirk, passing my best friend her next drink.

"Uh." She paused, eyes wide as she waited for me to get her out of this one.

"Piercings," I said matter-of-factly.

Naya spit her beer out in a straight projectile, her choking nearly enough to distract the simple little jock-brained boy standing next to her, hoping to get laid tonight.

"I think they would hurt, no?" her dimwitted date asked, not understanding the situation.

"Depends how you feel about pain." I winked, smiling big enough that my cheek piercings drew his attention.

She was right, though. Those lip rings could feel dangerously good in other places, and I needed a rebound.

Badly.

Naya giggled, hooking her arm into mine as we walked in front of Kyle and his friend, approaching our turn to enter the maze. I eyed my best friend's cup to make sure there was no floating sediment in her beer. I wouldn't put much past Kappa assholes.

We approached our turn, and a few in front of us were let into the maze followed by Kyle, his friend, and Naya. I handed the volunteer my ticket, but he shook his head, pulling the rope into place and sealing the entrance.

Naya's mouth went agape. "She's with us!"

"We can only let so many people in at once. Once a couple more come out, she can go in." They shrugged.

"Come on, we'll wait for her in there." Kyle pulled at Naya's hand, tugging her into his side and kissing her neck.

She giggled, pushing him off with barely enough time for her to mouth a 'sorry' to me as he threw her over his shoulder and pulled her into the maze.

Assholes.

I didn't resent her for it—she'd been drooling over Kyle for the last two years, and now that he'd finally returned the sentiment, I couldn't be upset that she was dropping everything for him, even if it was painfully obvious there was something insidious about his timing of interest and my breakup with his best friend. I couldn't prove it, and I wasn't about to ruin her chance to cross off a name on her bucket-fuck-list with my paranoid delusions about the world's maliciousness.

I shifted my weight from one foot to the other, crossing my arms impatiently as I tried to pretend to be invisible to the rest of the line behind me. There was something about being perceived as alone in public that rubbed me the wrong way. I knew damn well I came here with friends, but no one knew that right this second. They only saw me here, standing at the front of this line all by my lonesome with no one to talk to, and for some reason, that was a mortifying thought.

I pushed down the desire to walk through the line and tell every person one by one that I was, in fact, not alone.

"Are you always this anxious?" I heard from behind.

"Honestly, I'm surprised I haven't found a way to make money from it at this point," I retorted with a smile, glancing up to find my new lab partner.

Had he been behind us this whole time?

Holy shit, did he hear me and Naya talking about his piercings?

My face flushed with heat.

"You seemed fine in the lab." He peered down at me like he was studying me.

Was he here alone? He didn't seem to give a shit about how people perceived him. Damn, I'd spent far too much time with Noah, letting the opinions of his social circle dictate the strength of my self esteem.

"I'm comfortable in the lab. It's a safe space for me." I shrugged.

"There are no safe spaces," he said flatly. "Anything can happen anywhere at any time."

"True," I admitted, enjoying his refreshingly negative perspective. "But there are places where I'm not as afraid to be myself. Harkins' lab is one of those places."

His eyes narrowed. "Why's that?"

"There aren't hundreds of people watching me." I stated the obvious, shrugging my shoulders.

"You don't like being watched?" He gave a mischievous smirk.

I raised an eyebrow. "Depends on the context, I guess."

"Well, then." He leaned closer, his face moving toward mine at rapid speed, like he was about to kiss me. "I'll keep that in mind," he said, tucking a strand of hair behind my ear before stepping out of the line.

My lips parted, stunned with how forward every attractive man around me was suddenly acting now that I was single for the first time in three years.

"I'll see you in there." He nodded toward the maze before giving a two finger salute to the kid working the tickets.

The kid acknowledged him, and in one quick move, Zeke hopped over the stack of hay bales blocking the entrance to the maze.

"I thought you said it was full?" I whined to the kid.

"For paying visitors," he clarified.

What the fuck was that supposed to mean? I crossed my arms again, knowing there was no way in hell my best friend was still waiting for me at the entrance. She was likely getting railed by Danvers behind a stack of pumpkins somewhere in that maze. I'm sure if I listened closely, I could hear the faint sounds of his buddy high-fiving him for getting it on out there.

Maybe Naya was right.

Maybe all I needed was a rebound to cure this feeling.

It felt like an entire hour had gone by again before my turn had finally arrived. Kids rushed past me in line, screaming and laughing in frantic attempts to find the exit. *Left behind even by a group of children.*

Naya and Kyle were absolutely nowhere to be found, a heavy silence draped over the maze, bringing almost a paranormal feel to it. The fog was thick through the corn field, though whether it was natural or from some hidden machine was beyond me, but I didn't care to investigate further.

"Naya," I called out, not using my loudest yell, as if I was ashamed to be actually heard.

The audacity of me to try to find my people.

"Naya!" I called a little louder, this time cupping my hands around my mouth for an extra boost of volume.

A crow cawed out above me, like it was telling me to fuck off.

It was odd walking through here, the walls of corn so high and dense that they essentially blocked out any outside noise from the rest of the carnival.

Eerie as fuck.

I loved it.

Part of me had been partially bummed out when my new lab partner, Ezekiel, hopped over, leaving me alone. Some piece of me had been hoping we'd be grouped together, that by chance we'd end up having the perfect gothic meet-cute at a haunted corn maze attraction.

Never quite that lucky.

A scarecrow was perched atop a cross about five feet in the air in front of me. I didn't think they had the budget for those kinds of props, but damn, that thing looked like there could be someone in there. It was far too still, and I stood there, staring at it for way too long before deciding to move forward in the maze.

"Naya!" I called out again, this time with less effort.

The crow cawed like it was fucking following me, but I couldn't see it anywhere. One turn, then another, and I was sure I hadn't gone this way yet when I made that left, but there was the scarecrow again.

Or was it another?

How big was this fucking maze? No wonder it was taking hours for the line to move at all. People were going to go missing inside of this thing.

Maybe Naya and Kyle were just lost in some other corner, neither of them probably bright enough to figure out how to make it out of here, even if they combined their efforts. I'd been carrying Naya through most of her bachelor's degree, taking the tests in her online classes and writing whatever papers I could to ensure she'd pass.

It was what any best friend would do. Sure, there might have been a layer of enabling, but I wasn't responsible for the full weight of it; all I could do was help in the ways I knew how. It just meant that the ways I knew how consisted of passing her classes *for* her.

"Naya where the fuck are you?" I yelled, getting frustrated at the realization I'd been wandering this goddamn labyrinth for at least an hour, yet I wasn't any closer to finding my friend or the exit.

I stared up at the scarecrow again.

Was it a different one? It was impossible to tell if there were others in the distance—the wall of corn was far too high to see above it. I looked back up at the scarecrow; it wasn't like your regular, run-of-the-mill farm one. It was a burlap mask, made out of patches stitched together, draped over a head, a noose tightly strung around its neck to keep the 'stuffing' in place. Its mouth was sewn shut, and its eyes were dark holes impossible to see into. The stitches were a beige, skin-like color, almost resembling maggots thrown onto the scarecrow's badly formed face. A dark, hooded cape covered the rest of its body.

It was gnarly as fuck.

I stepped toward it, aching to inspect it from a closer distance. I could barely reach its foot from how high it was perched on the post.

I heard a shuffling in the corn, and I whipped my head to see if there was someone in this thicket with me.

"Naya?" I called out again, knowing damn well that bitch was far too loud to try to sneak up on me.

I gazed back at the scarecrow.

It was staring down directly at me.

Stumbling back in shock, I tripped over my own feet, falling onto the ground.

"Fuck," I cursed, catching myself with my elbows to keep from falling further onto my ass. The shock buzzed through both of my arms, and a slew of my favorite curses flew from my tongue as I rubbed myself for warmth.

That's when the scarecrow dropped its arms from the cross before coming to a knee on the post as it stared at me. My heart thumped quickly just beneath my throat as he jumped down onto the ground in front of me, and a scream forced its way from my mouth involuntarily.

Damn scare actors. I thought it was a fucking prop.

How many times had this asshole watched me walk by, screaming for Naya?

His head moved just slightly at an angle.

"Look at you. Pretty little darkling, all alone in this big, empty corn maze." He was using a voice changer.

I stayed frozen as, one step after another, he moved closer, lazily, like he was in no rush to get to me.

"There's no way out of here, you know that, right?" the scarecrow said with a chuckle.

"That seems like a fire hazard. There's got to be at least one way." I grinned, pushing myself up to my feet and moving closer to him. "Are you gonna tell me where it is?" I whispered into the mask.

"You seem to think you have any say here." He tried to disarm me once again, hovering over me with far too little care for my personal space.

"What's the alternative?" I pushed at his shoulder, as if I could move him from my way, but the scarecrow was more like a heavy brick wall than a bag of hay.

A husky growl came from the depths of the disturbing mask, leather gloves gripping at my shoulders as the scarecrow walked me into a wall of maze. I gasped, startled at the way he was able to overpower and move me with so little effort.

His knee split my legs apart as he got impossibly closer, his mask pressing into my face in an attempt to intimidate me.

"I want to see you scurry through this labyrinth like the rest of them. I want you to beg me to release you." His leathered thumbs rubbed slow circles against the front of my shoulders.

I could smell the mint of his gum through the mask, and my brain immediately made the connection for me. I knew faculty were forced to volunteer in these fundraiser events, but the thought of Harkins here, in this mask, with a chance for something physical and human, had need burning through me.

"What if I just beg you for release?" I breathed out, grinding against his thigh.

I closed my eyes, biting my bottom lip as I reveled in the momentary bliss. He lifted his leg to ease my motion, aiding in my pleasure, though only through friction.

"Fuck." The scarecrow's disguised voice breathed over me, his hands moving to my hips as he gripped tightly, moving me against his leg. "Ask me to come," he commanded.

I shook my head, biting at my lip as I antagonized him with my disobedience.

He squeezed my hips, forcing all movement to a stop until I'd give him what he wanted.

My brain said fight, but my pussy said, 'we deserve this'.

"Let me come," I begged, my panties soaked with desire and my clit swollen with need.

Rough leather gloves found their way between my thighs, disregarding my skirt as he pushed aside my panties. He slipped his fingers between my folds, now slick and dripping all over his pants. My breathing hitched at his touch, but I stayed frozen, waiting for him to make a move, any move.

It didn't count if we pretended like it wasn't him. He wasn't doing anything wrong.

We weren't teacher and student in this moment.

We were just two people giving into a human need.

Electrifying.

Each stroke of his fingers against my most sensitive spots had stars blinding me, colorful spots swimming across my vision from how tightly I squeezed my eyelids shut. Gripping his costume, I held on to him as one hand continued to guide my hips, the other rubbing over my clit with care.

I dropped my head against his chest as the feeling grew, a wave of pleasure threatening to crash over me and pull me under. His fingers pinched then pulled, forcing a cry from my lips at the shock jolting through my very bones.

"Fuck, Camila," the scarecrow breathed as I bit his chest through his costume, anchoring myself as my body prepared to give out from the intensity of the orgasm shredding me apart.

I opened my eyes to oblivion, his face too dark through the costume to see anything or make out any features.

"Next time, I'll have you over my cock, stretching out that pretty cunt of yours." He wiped his hand over the mess on his pants before turning away.

"Hey, wait. Give me at least a hint," I said, still breathy and high from my climax.

He tilted his head toward the passage on the right of us before disappearing into the wall of corn.

Fuck.

FIVE
WITH SCARECROWS
LIKE THESE

"Naya!" I tried again, sounding more pathetic than before, knowing that bitch had abandoned me.

My feet were starting to hurt, and the sun had long set. It was pitch black, and I was trying to conserve the flashlight on my phone to keep my battery from dying.

This shit was not well organized, and it was going to be at least three in the morning before they'd get everyone out.

"You look lost." I recognized the familiar sound of the voice changer and whipped my head to look for the scarecrow.

There was no perch, and there was no one near.

"Harkins?" I whispered, my heart once again beating louder than my words.

The possibility of running into him again in this maze was one I had been praying for.

"I saw you moaning with his fingers in your cunt," I heard through the voice changer again.

I turned around, expecting to see someone, but once again, I found myself alone. "Who the fuck is there?"

"I'm right here." It felt like he was practically in my ear—an unsettling notion, but by the time I turned again, there was no one there.

I stepped quickly, moving through the maze. Someone was fucking with me. Someone saw us, and they were going to do something about it. Would they try to get Harkins fired? I couldn't remember which way I'd come from and, one left turn after another, I'd found myself at a dead end, completely trapped, with no way out.

Picking up the pace, I panted heavily with every step as I rushed through sections of the labyrinth I could no longer recognize. Boots crunched around me, but I couldn't pinpoint their exact location. In front of me? Next to me? Somehow, it sounded like it was everywhere. It was too dark, too disorienting, and if not for the stars above me, I'd have lost all sense of direction.

I tripped over something spilt on the ground, sending me flying face first. Before the ground could meet me, though, arms wrapped around my waist, lifting me up and steadying me back onto my feet.

"Was I not supposed to see? Is that not why you did it right in front of me, Camila?" the voice said again, right in my ear.

I turned to find him gone.

"Who-Where are you?" I asked, masking the shakiness in my voice with the illusion of authority.

"Right here," he hissed in my ear, forcing me to jerk my head to the side on instinct.

"Goddamnit!" I yelled, frustrated that someone was playing mind games with me.

"You smell delicious, little darkling. Good enough to eat." It sounded like a threat, but nonetheless, the words registered deep in my core.

It reminded me of what my professor had just done to me.

"What do you want?" I spun around to find nothing but corn behind me.

I heard the dull sound of two feet hitting the ground. "I want what you gave him."

The wind blew through my hair, caressing the skin normally shielded by raven strands. I forced my body to still, ignoring the shiver rippling through my spine. I didn't dare turn to face him yet.

"What I gave to who?" I shifted my eyes to my peripheral, hoping I'd catch a glimpse of whoever was behind me.

He stepped closer, too close, his body pressed against my back. I fought to keep from shaking, but it was useless. Strong hands gripped my shoulders from behind, squeezing until I felt a sharp pain.

"Your teacher." My body tensed up, still trapped in his hold but not daring to face him.

"I don't know what you're talking about," I whispered into the dark abyss of the maze.

"Don't lie to me, little darkling." There was a sharpness to his tone I could hear even through the changer.

I shifted my weight uncomfortably between my feet.

"Why are you so..." He paused, as if he was calculating his next word. "Anxious?"

My breath hitched and caught like a bubble in my chest.

I didn't respond.

"Answer me, Camila." His demand was laced with authority, even through the voice changer.

"You're threatening me." I couldn't help the anger in my voice, the thought that just an hour ago, a stranger had witnessed me vulnerable, caught in a moment of complicated bliss and emotions with a man I'd admired as a mentor for the last two years.

A moment I had been secretly wishing for in the back of my mind even in a devoted, monogamous relationship.

He was going to use it against me.

"Did I say that?" He cut through my thoughts as if he could hear them.

"Then what do you want?" I snapped, my teeth clinking together in annoyance.

A dark chuckle filled the space around us, his hands releasing my shoulders.

"I want to play with my food before I eat it." The voice lingered, suspended in the air, belonging to no one and coming from nowhere all at once.

What did that mean? What the fuck did he want from me?

"Run, darkling. Run as fast as you can," he thundered in my ears.

A sharp scream filled the air in the distance, setting off a violent drumming in my heart.

My feet moved beneath me, no message from my brain to my body necessary. I ran, faster than ever before, only slowing down when the abrupt dead ends of the maze forced me to turn and find another way.

Where the fuck was Naya?

Where the fuck was *anything*?

Sweat beaded at my temple before trickling down the side of my face, my stomach cramping from the most exercise my body had seen in at least a decade.

"Don't be scared, little darkling," his voice found me again.

"I'm not scared," I lied. I *was* scared.

Scared of what he could do to Harkins' career, my reputation.

Scared of a man? Of something made of flesh and bone and weakness? Not so much.

But this game, this chase, was igniting something deep inside me that my body so desperately craved.

The give and take, the control and surrender.

It could be addicting.

"Play my game, little darkling." The scarecrow's voice circled around me.

"What do you want?" I bit back.

"Run. Run until you make it out." This time, his voice wasn't masked by the voice changer, a hint of familiarity tugging at my brain.

"That sounds exhausting." I said, not bothering to hide my annoyance. I shifted my weight again, "What happens if I get out?"

"Then your little secret...dies with me." I felt his breath in my ear.

"And if I don't?" I asked.

"If I catch you, then you're mine to play with." He chuckled.

My legs trembled beneath me, "For how long?" I asked.

"For as long as I want." His real voice broke through the voice changer again, but I still couldn't place it.

His words sent cold panic through my entire body.

"I'll give you a head start, and I'll even point you in the right direction." A lantern lit up in the distance, showing an opening through the stalks of maize.

"One," he counted. I stepped slowly toward the light.

"Two." My heart thumped louder, his voice distant as I moved to the illuminated path.

I picked up the lantern, not missing the opportunity to preserve what little battery I had left on my phone.

"Three." There was too much electricity in the air, and I moved faster than before, a new wave of energy coursing through my body out of pure self-preservation.

I'd worked too hard for this life to let someone take it all away from me, to trash my name because I made a stupid mistake, as if no one else had ever fucked up before and an example needed to be made of me for all to see.

Bile surged its way up my throat, but I swallowed it down, my feet stomping with urgent need as a faint 'four' vibrated in the distance.

I needed to find the way out.

Yet, some sick, twisted, part of me wondered if I'd like to be caught just the same.

SIX
AND NOW, FOR A TWIST

"Dude, where the fuck are you? I've been calling and texting you for hours." She sounded pissed, as if she wasn't the one who completely ditched me.

"I've been stuck in this maze looking for you, asshole. I barely get any service from being in bum fuck nowhere. Throw these ten feet corn stalks in the mix, and I don't even have a single missed call. You've probably just been fucking Kyle in a porta-potty."

"You're still in the maze, Mila? Kyle, she's still in the maze. Go get the cops." Her panic made my heart beat faster.

"What are you freaking out about?" I steadied my voice, knowing if I showed a glimmer of anxiety, she'd unravel.

"Some kid went fucking psycho in the maze and started killing people! The carnival is filled with cops, and they said they emptied the maze, but they're afraid of sending too many cops inside because it's so hard to get out. It looks like all the people who knew how to get out got killed." The pause on the other end of the line was heavy, even though I knew it was my turn to respond.

My arms suddenly turned into lead, the sound of her voice becoming distant as I dropped the phone from my hand.

"Mila! Mila!" I could hear the faint shouts from the phone.

How the fuck was I going to get out of here?

SEVEN
THIS CHAPTER IS PURE SMUT

I slowed down, confident I'd put some distance between us this time. My heart still fluttered violently in my chest while I did my best to keep track of every turn I'd taken. I should have left that stupid lantern on the ground, kept it as a marker to make sure I wasn't going in circles.

I was definitely going in circles.

I'd found myself in a familiar spot, the perch and cross with a scarecrow high above me looming menacingly.

I turned away from it, unsure if this one was a prop by the way it hung lazily from the stake. With my head turned, looking behind me, I ran forward. I was stopped abruptly, choking, wheezing from the feel of a hard wall knocking the wind from my lungs. I turned to face the scarecrow, the noose over the mask, the smell of mint gum in the air.

I looked back to find the perch was now empty.

"I've been looking for you everywhere," I heard through the voice changer, a drop of panic somehow recognizable through the camouflage of the machine.

"Demetri—Dr. Harkins?" I asked, breathless, the hope in my chest expansive, draping my body in a warm surge of comfort.

He wrapped his arms around me, pulling me in tightly. There was a desperation to his embrace, a fear I could feel through his touch, as if what had happened between us earlier was going to be more than just a regret.

"I need to get you out of here. We need to go, Camila." He pulled the mask off, dropping it to the ground beneath us.

He had always been handsome enough to steal the air from my lungs, but with his hair disheveled from the burlap mask, there was something even more desirable about him. This new air of protectiveness he wore was enough to make me believe in fairytale happy endings.

Or had it always been there?

I thought back to every time I'd shown up to class with swollen, red eyes, how Harkins would somehow find a way to 'make my day worse' by slamming me with extra work and unnecessary research he suddenly had impossible deadlines for. He somehow understood that the best way for my brain to deal with what my emotions couldn't handle was by simply distracting me with a harder task.

He'd keep me after labs for review discussions on days he knew I'd be in my dorm all alone while Noah would be celebrating a football victory with his Kappas. Fidelity from your boyfriend was never an expectation when dating a fraternity brother, and he'd somehow become my place of comfort, the one I instinctively went to anytime I had a problem I couldn't solve myself.

Now, here he was again.

I wanted to be the one to protect him, to keep that asshole from ruining everything Demetri had built for himself at our school. Every thought melted from my mind once his hand cupped the side of my face, warm and reassuring.

I leaned into his touch.

Another piercing scream shot off in the distance, penetrating deep into my bones.

Then, silence again.

My eyes didn't dare waver from his, obsidian in the night aside from the glimmering speckles of light that reflected the sky. His forehead pressed to mine and before I could speak, the warmth of his lips found me. My free hand gripped his chest, fingertips straining to hold on to his clothing as his tongue ravaged its way inside my mouth.

His free hand slid down my side, curving behind me as he grabbed my ass and pulled me against him. "Do you feel that?" he growled in my ear as the hard steel of his cock stabbed against my belly. "I've been like this since I got to taste your cum off my gloves."

Hot lava seeped its way down to my core, forcing my thighs to clamp shut to relieve some of the need to feel his touch again.

"I want to feel you," I whispered, sounding more like a plea.

I dropped the lantern, my hands shaking with nerves as I reached for his belt buckle using the faint flicker of the light below us. His hands stayed on me, fingers gripping my ass tightly with a bruising pressure as his other hand moved from my face to my neck, holding the side of my throat. His lips never stopped, his tongue exploring my mouth like he'd been waiting his whole life to get to know it.

A whimper caught in my throat as my hands found their way into his pants, his cock too thick, and unbelievably hard.

For me.

He pulled his lips from mine. "You have no idea how long I've wanted to do this."

I squeezed the base of his cock, a groan leaving his mouth as I pulled him from his pants. My mouth watered at the sight; even in the dim light, I could see the outline of how thick it was. My hand would never wrap all the way around.

I dropped to my knees, unprepared for the spiky ends of the hay to stab so viciously into my skin. I adjusted, blocking out the pain as I parted my lips and took my professor's cock into my mouth.

"Fuck," he hissed, both of his hands gripping my hair tightly as I swirled my tongue around the head.

A salty bead of pre-cum trickled over my tastebuds. I moaned, savoring his taste as I licked the underside of his shaft all the way down to the base, squeezing tightly again with my other hand before I licked my way back up. I looked up at him, unable to see anything but the depth of his eyes and the dimples in his cheeks from the smile he must have been wearing.

"I'm tired of holding back, Camila," he confessed.

There was something about the way he said it, like it was more than just about this very moment. I nodded, unsure if he could see my agreement before I opened my mouth to take all of him.

He was so fucking big, the corners of my lips hurt from spreading wide to make room for him, but I tried anyway, pulling back and licking at my lips before trying again to devour this beast.

The heat between my legs begged for release, but in the back of my mind, I was officially afraid. Afraid of the Coke can that was going to split me in half.

Fuck it, I'd die trying.

His hands pulled at my hair, forcing him deeper down my throat. I could feel the corners of my mouth splitting, tiny little cuts that would prove to be the only evidence of what we'd done here tonight.

I was reveling in the sound of his pleasure, his moans of bliss stuttering from his throat as he called my name everytime I pulled back before sucking him deeper down my throat. It was impossible to move my tongue; there was no room in my mouth with him occupying all the space, but whatever I was doing seemed to be enough.

Drool leaked freely past my lips down to my chin.

"Looks like the wrong scarecrow caught you first, little dark-ling," a voice called from behind.

I could feel Demetri's body tense, and sweat collected at the back of my neck from the sound of that voice changer.

"Who the fuck is there?" Harkins shouted into the darkness, nothing but our little bubble of illumination revealing our sur-roundings.

"Put your mask back on, *professor*," the scarecrow command-ed. "Don't want anyone to see you here, with a *student*."

Demetri Harkins stepped in front of me, stuffing himself back into his pants before making himself somehow larger, as if attempting to cover me with his body.

Like he was protecting me from this creep's malicious stares.

He reached down to grab the mask and put it back over his head.

"We're gonna play a little game now," the scarecrow said, coming into view as he stepped toward us.

"I *know* what you've been doing in this maze, Camila," he spoke, his mask nearly identical to the professor's.

"I don't know what you mean." I feigned ignorance, know-ing it would be my only weapon.

Aside from the pocket-knife tucked inside my Doc Martens.

"Stand behind her," the scarecrow commanded the other.

Demetri growled under his breath but, feeling the unrelent-ing weight of the situation , he moved behind me again as the other walked around us in slow circles like a predator, calculating his next move.

"I played your game," I said through gritted teeth. "What more do you want?"

"We haven't finished the game," he laughed. "I just caught you. Now, you're mine. You both are." There was a psychotic type of joy emphasized by the voice changer when he laughed.

Hands found my waist, squeezing as he groped and felt my body like he was inspecting a piece of meat at the market.

There was a thrill in all of this that I couldn't describe, couldn't make sense of. When I ran face first into Dr. Harkins, a part of me had hoped it was the other scarecrow, that I had been caught and the lingering promise would be fulfilled, that the *real* fun would start.

My disappointment was tampered by the taste of Demetri on my tongue and his cock splitting open my mouth. Now, here we were again, not just me, but the both of us, flies in his web.

The worst part was, I was desperate to know what he'd do.

I could feel my pussy dripping with the need to find out.

"Our little darkling is lost in this big maze. Let's show her how well the corn keeps the screams from escaping," the voice said from behind, reaching inside my shirt to cup a breast.

A growl came from Harkins, his possessiveness affecting his ability to process this situation.

As if all that mattered was me.

"Touch her," Zeke commanded Demetri from below me, like he'd dropped to his knees.

It was too dark to see who was touching me and where. Their individual scents mingled and invaded my senses together, citrus, cedar, and smoke with a dash of mint. Leathered gloves rubbed up my thighs, splitting my legs apart before I felt a hot breath against my pussy.

He'd taken his mask off.

A hot, wet tongue lapped its way up my center. The cold metal of two steel balls from his piercings was a startling feeling that impulsively had me clenching my thighs together, smashing his head in the process. My knees buckled as he continued, fighting against my thighs. I moaned, reaching down for his shoulders, looking for some sort of support, but instead, I was pulled back by Demetri's strong hands as he held me flush against his body.

It was like this was his way of conceding to this, but still maintaining control, still having some sort of say, and he was saying he was going to have me regardless. He pinned my arms behind my back with a single hand as the other moved to rub my nipples, slow circles with the occasional pinch that drove me insane.

I was a river of pleasure flowing directly through both of them, a waterfall of proof spilling onto the tongue of the man beneath me, his fingers gripping my thighs while he voraciously devoured me. I quivered with every flick of his double-pierced tongue against my swollen clit, my cunt aching with the need to be filled but my body giving out and accepting this pleasure as it were. The orgasm ripped through me, my arousal dripping down my thighs while I seized in my professor's hold.

I finally looked down to see the lantern's flame bouncing off Ezekiel's shadowed face beneath me. I was still quivering from the aftershocks of pleasure when the realization of his identity set in.

In a way, I almost knew it hadn't been Demetri, but what did he have to gain from this?

My brain twisted and stretched inside my skull, trying to manipulate some sort of answer that would feel real enough, justifiable for these actions.

Remembering the call with my best friend, my heart began to race again while I tried to conjure a way out of this labyrinth.

"We're not done," his voice cut through my thoughts.

Harkins' hold on me tightened protectively, his exhale in my ear sending goosebumps down my neck before he whispered, "There's a killer in the maze." I froze.

He knew there was a killer in the maze. Did Demetri think Ezekiel's goal was to blackmail us into fucking him? That we were possibly the next victims? I looked back down at the devastatingly beautiful face beneath me.

I knew exactly what I'd need to do to get out of here now.

And I was really going to enjoy it, too.

"Put your fingers in her ass. I want her ready to fuck both of us." Zeke's announcement was nearly as abrupt as the two fingers he slid inside my pussy.

They were long, reaching deep, his knuckles caressing as he explored my body. I whimpered, needy for more but unable to vocalize my demands.

That's when Harkins' fingers joined Ezekiel's. They were much thicker, shorter, but equally as effective as the two dueled between my legs for dominance.

To see who could make me unravel faster.

"Oh fuck," I gasped, my mind going blank as everything but their fingers stopped mattering.

My arms were tingling behind my back from the pressure of Demetri's hold, but the idea of both of them fucking me at once was enough to make me drool through lazy, parted lips as they found a rhythm. They took turns hitting my g-spot so that the pressure was constant, unrelenting, and the next orgasm took me down without mercy.

"Oh God!" I cried out as my cum gushed down my legs.

"Don't insult me, Camila. A girl like you gave up believing in God a long time ago." Ezekiel hooked his fingers inside me, using it to pull my pussy closer to his face.

That pierced tongue found its way between my legs again, cleaning the mess I'd made from their joint work. Demetri let out a content hum in my ear, softly whispering, "So good, so obedient." I purred from the praise, melting into his grip, so solid and heavy around me.

My arms were slightly numb from the way he held them back, but my mind was soon distracted by the feel of his fingers toying with the entrance of my ass. He rubbed around the delicate, puckered ring, a cry stumbling from my lips at how heightened every sensation felt after so many orgasms.

"Please," I begged, my voice a pathetic whimper as my ass tilted upwards.

The lantern's fire dimmed, so quickly and so abruptly that the world darkened again, aside from the stars.

"Greedy little darkling," I heard in front of me before the sound of a zipper pierced the air. "Tell our professor how badly you want us both to fill you up, to stretch your holes and pump you full of our cum until you leave a trail behind you through this maze."

Harkins growled behind me, his fingers still teasing the entrance of my ass.

He needed to know, he needed to understand. His fingers slid inside me again, collecting lubricant before pressing against my puckered hole.

"I-I do," I confessed. "I want you both." At once, two of Demetri's thick fingers pushed through the tight barrier, filling me from behind.

I gasped, backing into him to deepen the sensation.

Ezekiel let out a slow, dark chuckle before lifting up my right leg and dropping it over his arm. The head of his cock pressed against my clit, the cold steel of a curved barbell forcing my eyes wide from surprise. He rubbed up and down, my standing leg shaking from the overwhelming sensation.

"Fuck!" I cried out as he took his time entering me, savoring every inch of the experience.

"Did I beat you to it, professor?" There was a smugness to his tone, like he was reveling in knowing he took something from Demetri. "She's sopping wet. I bet I could fit my whole arm inside her."

I couldn't respond, couldn't deny or confirm while every stroke of his cock buried deeper inside me, his piercing rubbing against me in the most delicious way while Demetri's fingers worked in harmony from behind to drive me to madness.

Harkins didn't answer him, didn't allow Ezekiel's goading to push him over the edge. He knew he was the better man. He didn't need to react.

"You're perfect, Mila," he whispered softly in my ear, making sure it stayed between the two of us.

Our secret.

"Fuck her ass, Harkins," Zeke growled in frustration as he thrusted into me, each time harder than the last.

"I can't, I won't fit," he admitted in a way that expressed zero shame about his size.

Good. That thing was a masterpiece, an instrument of God, and I couldn't wait to feel it inside of me.

His response only forced Ezekiel's pace to quicken, as if his only goal now was his own release.

Demetri's hand released mine, a buzzing sensation trickling through my arms as I reached behind to hang on to him by my own choice. With my right hand on his shoulder and my left using his neck for support, my nails dug into his skin as Zeke moved inside of me.

I cried with the need for release, driven solely to be a vessel for the pleasure I was given no choice but to surrender myself to.

"Please," I whined, unsure for what, but the words fell out of me anyway.

"She's begging you for it," Zeke assured him, though he hadn't seen what Harkins was working with yet.

"No," he gritted out, his voice sinking to a deep register I'd never heard in the two years I'd known him.

I squirmed against his fingers, unmoving since they'd used up the little lubricant I'd provided. I was so close to the edge again, desperate for another orgasm, even though I was practically boneless, a limp fuck-doll desperate to be filled and defiled by the two men pressed against me.

One of whom I'd known for a total of twelve hours.

And he was blackmailing me into fucking both him and my professor.

When the words finally formed into a cohesive thought, it really was a wild realization. So, I let the corners of my lips turn up into a smile, letting my body enjoy every inch of this moment.

"You seem to think that I'm asking, professor. I am not. Fuck her in the ass if you want to leave this maze with your career intact." The threat was loud and clear, but it was Demetri who didn't back down.

His fingers withdrew from inside me, a hollow feeling that left me uncomfortably needy for more. With a solid push of his hand against Ezekiel's chest, I was left completely empty as the professor took him down. Demetri was shorter than him, but what he may have lacked in height, he made up for in build. Zeke fell back to the ground where I could no longer see him, but I could see the outline of the professor hovering over him.

"I'm not hurting her so you can get your rocks off over it. You want my cock involved so bad, have at it yourself," he seethed, pulling himself out of his pants. By the glory of God, the moon peeked out from behind the clouds, illuminating this beautiful moment for us all to witness.

Zeke's mouth parted at the sight of the professor's cock, his mouth pulling up in a smirk as he took it in.

"Well, well, well," he chuckled. "You're a big boy, aren't you, professor?" He moved to his knees, licking his bottom lip. His eyes never straying from Demetri's cock, hypnotized by it.

I inched closer, dropping to my knees for the perfect position to observe. Zeke grabbed him by the base of his shaft, a hiss leaving Demetri's mouth, as if he wasn't expecting such firmness. I had been afraid to handle it, softly gripping, like I could somehow damage him.

Ezekiel, however, squeezed tightly, unafraid to teeter a point that looked like it could dance the edge of pain. Harkins dropped his head back, moaning at the feel of Zeke's tongue swirling madly around the head of his cock.

I pressed my thighs together. Ezekiel's pre-cum drying on my flesh was nearly as itchy as the sharp hay that poked and shoved its way into the crevices of my clothing, but I couldn't stop watching. I was enthralled by the carnal heat of the moment, that this was no longer just about me, but about everyone's pleasure, about giving and taking and letting go.

Ezekiel looked to be having a harder time than I had opening up to take him. "Just relax," I encouraged him. "It's easier if you're not stretching your lips so tight."

His right hand gripped his own cock while his left moved up and down Demetri's shaft. He slurped and licked like he was just as hungry for it as I was, and I bit my lip, wishing my turn hadn't been interrupted.

As if my thoughts had been said out loud, Zeke shifted his stare my way for just a moment, finding I had moved right next to him. His hand moved up and down, his cock freely leaking as he deepthroated our professor as best he could.

My fingers danced their way between my legs to alleviate the need to feel just as good. I slid them between my folds, gasping at the realization of how wet and messy it was down there. I groaned, too loudly, and both men shifted to look at me. I shook my head, a silent command that this wasn't over yet. Instead, I leaned forward, joining Zeke in devouring the tasty treat in front of us.

I licked up the bottom of his shaft, the spit dripping from Ezekiel's now-practiced slurping joining with mine as we coated Demetri's cock in our saliva. He moaned, one hand dropping to each of our heads as he pulled us closer to him than I thought possible.

"I'm going to come," he warned, pulling Zeke further down his cock, pushing me away with a soft caress.

He wasn't gentle like he was with me, choking him on his length as Zeke pressed against his thighs to try to push back. Harkins only pulled him further down his shaft, the raspy choking sounds only relieved by the short bursts of gagging as his vomit fought to rise up his throat.

He was so uncomfortable, and Harkins didn't give a fuck. I rubbed against my clit, moaning in sync with him as he face-fucked his newest student. The pleasure built inside me quickly, more from the scene playing out in front of me than what I was doing to myself. It was the hottest thing I'd ever seen in my life.

I came, crying out for Demetri and finding his eyes glued to mine as he spilled his cum down Ezekiel's throat. Once his grip relaxed, Zeke pushed away, scrambling backwards as he coughed uncontrollably.

"You fucking asshole!" he rasped, rubbing his throat as he made inhuman noises, trying to catch his breath again.

I cackled, throwing my head back at the sight.

I looked up at Demetri to find him smirking at me.

"Does the professor know you've been out here, cutting frat boys from throat to dick?" he spat at me, like he was happy to be the one spilling my secrets.

Demetri's smirk softened, but it wasn't a look of fear I found in his face.

"Who do you think has been hiding the bodies out there in the corn?" he responded, his gaze staying fixed on mine.

"Demetri," I gasped, unable to hide my surprise.

"I saw the videos. I saw what Noah's friends did to you." A line creased between his eyebrows as his anger grew more evident. "If it had been me, I would have done far worse to them," he threatened.

His fingers found mine, and a gentle squeeze was all I needed to settle any fear that grew in my heart.

I stepped forward, and he followed right behind.

"Lick her boots," he commanded his student, deep, self-assured authority dripping from his voice that had me practically puffing my own chest out with pride.

I didn't turn back, smiling at his demand.

"Lick her boots." The professor's voice darkened to a fearsome tone as he repeated himself through gritted teeth, grabbing Ezekiel by the back of the head and tossing him at my feet.

Zeke looked up at me like it was an outrageous demand. It was nothing I'd ever thought of, had never desired, but I couldn't lie: the thought of seeing him on his knees, licking my boots clean, was doing something between my legs.

He dropped his head in defeat before lowering himself all the way down to the ground, his tongue flicking out slowly to lick from the toe to the side of my Doc Martens.

"You can do better than that," the professor declared. "Try again." He chuckled. "With gusto this time."

I heard a grunt of displeasure beneath me, Zeke's tongue pressing down flat against the toe of my boot, licking the leather like an ice cream cone.

"Oh, do that again." I dropped my head back in pleasure, the sight alone enough to make me reach between my legs. I slipped my hand into my skirt and past my panties to fight to get myself off again.

"Again," Harkins growled like a guard dog.

Once more, the flat of his tongue ran from the front to the side of my boot, this time running up the zipper on the outside. Once he looked back up at me, I pulled my fingers from my skirt, licking each one clean before giving him my attention.

I sent my boot straight down onto his face, kicking him into a pile of hay.

EIGHT
WE LOVE A CHASE SCENE

Zeke

"You're fucking nuts. You're all fucking nuts in this town!" I scratched out, panic lacing what could be heard of my voice as I crab-walked backwards in a hurry.

I hit a bale of hay behind me, loose straw covering me from above as they infiltrated every inch of my costume, embedding into my skin. I jerked from the burn of discomfort, twisting my neck to see I was cornered by the girl on one side.

Pulling the knife from inside of her leather boots, her chin jerked back up at me, an eerie smile stretching over her face.

Harkins zipped his pants, confidently walking toward me, boxing me in from the other side now that he'd confirmed I wasn't the threat, now that he knew *she* wasn't the one in danger. I'd just transferred to NPC, a favor pulled by my great aunt, who was retiring out of the Botany department this year. Faculty were supposed to work this event, but my great aunt no longer had the knees for this kind of bullshit.

I kindly offered to take her place.

The minute I saw Camila in line, I thought some strings of fate were being pulled in our direction, that I'd get a chance to make a move on a girl who was almost too beautiful to be real. Then, I saw her coming with our professor's fingers in her cunt.

It was so fucking hot, and I couldn't get the sight out of my mind. I thought I could use what I'd seen, what I knew, to manipulate them into a night we would all enjoy, a night we could all leave behind here.

Then, she killed some kid in a football jersey, and then another. Now, I'd realized fucking with this girl might have been the worst idea I'd ever had in my life.

"Are you done with him?" Harkins asked her, reaching down for my throat.

His teeth glimmered in the light, like a predator ready to howl at the moon. Fingers wrapped tightly around my neck, he applied even more pressure. I scratched out, but his strength was greater than mine. Colorful dots swam over my vision as my blood flow and oxygen were cut off, no thought of mercy to be found anywhere on his face.

"No, he had his fun. I think we should get to have ours now, don't you?" she asked in a voice so innocent, it could only be a farce.

She split her hair down the middle with ease, skillfully twisting ropes of hair until two braids hung down to her waist. She squatted down in front of me, one knee on the ground as the other splayed out widely, purposefully displaying her messy, still dripping cunt to me. Harkins growled under his breath, squeezing harder and forcing my chin up so I no longer had access to that marvelous sight.

She smiled a wicked grin.

Licking the tip of her knife and twirling it on her tongue before she brought it down to graze the center of my chest, she pressed just hard enough to scratch the surface of my skin. I grunted, less bothered by my suffering than the discomfort of realizing I had fucked with a broken woman. Now, I was truly headed for the unpredictable.

"He likes the chase," she hummed, one hand pulling on the end of a braid while the other twirled the knife over her knee. "Maybe we should let him see what it's like to be the prey." She looked up at Harkins, a malicious smile draped over his face.

"L-let me go. I promise I wasn't going to tell anyone." I tried to reason with her, but everytime the clouds uncovered the moon, the light exposed the blood painting her from nearly head to toe.

"She's beautifully macabre," Harkins prosed, describing the wild banshee in front of us.

"She's a fucking psycho," I corrected him.

A scream ripped through my throat, a burning agony in my foot forced me to look down to see her knife had made its way into the center of it. I wailed, screeching but unable to move, as my foot had been pinned to the ground by her knife.

"Fuck! Fuck!" I rasped out, Harkins making no effort to soften his hold on my throat as I writhed in pain like an insect pinned to a board while still alive.

"You thought you could use our moment of weakness for your enjoyment," she said, all that sinister sweetness devoid from her tone.

"Take that knife out of my foot, you fucking crazy bitch!" I shouted, but she cackled in response.

She spat at my face, the glob landing inside my mouth and over my eyes. "Oh, I'm sorry, does it hurt?" she mocked, pulling the knife out, but before I could even cradle my injured foot, she'd stabbed the knife into the other.

Another scream tore through my throat, uncaring of the pressure from Harkins' hand as the burn of the knife crushed through my bones. My head was spinning, my body shaking and trembling from the stinging ache, my brain unable to process which foot to focus on. When I thought she would pull the knife out, she instead twisted it, an unrecognizable scream pummeling its way out of my throat.

"You aren't going to get away with this," I panted, sweat dripping down my back as I fought my body from going into shock.

My teeth snapped, clicking loudly as she pulled the knife out once more. No ounce of shame was left in my body to prevent the violent chattering as I succumbed to the agony she mercilessly bestowed. Her eyes were moonless, darker than I'd ever noticed them to be, and when she leaned into the ray of moonlight, I could see the evil embedded deep into her soul.

She'd always been this way.

She was henbane, beautiful but foul in every sense of the word; the closer you got, the more evident it became as its stench invaded your senses. She was wretched, toxic in the worst way possible, but stunningly beautiful from a distance.

I should have left her at that distance, because someone like her was never meant for someone like me. I looked up at Dr. Harkins through my blurred, teary vision. He was looking at her like she was the entire universe, like she was his whole reason for breathing.

Fucking lunatics.

She leaned forward, whispering into my ear, "I already got away with it."

She stood up, stepping back, and with a gesture of her head, Harkins did the same.

"I'll give you a head start," she whispered, twirling the tip of the knife on the pad of her index finger.

"One," Harkins counted, her eyes going wide with enthusiasm at his desire to play along.

I stumbled back, using the hay to support me as I attempted to stand. My feet burned beneath me, forcing me to drop to my knees with a pained cry.

"Two," she dragged out with the same, sickly-sweet fake voice she'd used before.

I looked up to see them staring down at me, sinister smiles painted on their faces as they watched me struggle. I bit my cheeks through the pain, knowing there was no way to avoid the torture, that giving up would likely cost me my life.

I had one thing going for me.

I knew the way out.

I tried to stand again, biting hard enough to taste liquid metal over my tongue as I masked my misery in front of my predators.

"Three," Harkins sneered menacingly.

I hobbled past them, doing my best to take large but fast steps to distribute the throbbing ache. Tears streamed down my face, though I clenched my jaw shut to avoid crying out from the suffering. I moved as fast as I could, only stopping once Camila's 'four' sounded safely enough in the distance for me to drop to my knees and crawl.

I could get out of here.

This place was littered with cops. All I had to do was make it out of the maze.

All I had to do was make it out of the maze, I repeated in my head like a silent prayer, convincing myself I'd be able to do it. The sharpness in my feet never dulled, even as they became heavy weights, anchoring me back as I drug my knees across the hay. It stabbed the palms of my hands, itching as it crawled up my sleeves while I desperately scuffled toward my next left turn.

"Five," Harkins' voice boomed out.

I froze, a cold wind brushing the back of my neck, the dry sweat sending a chill down my spine.

"Please, God, if I make it out of here..." I began to bargain, not knowing what promises I was yet willing to make to save my ass from whatever death she'd planned for me.

"God's not listening," I heard her whisper in the wind.

"Six," she called back from a further distance.

I dragged myself forward, shuffling on all fours as fast as I could manage.

"Just let me go! Please!" I begged loudly, hoping my cries would somehow reach the outside.

A sharp sting slashed through the back of my ankle, the wet of the blood trickling freely down the side of my foot, letting me know my achilles tendon had been sliced. A feral screech passed through my lips before I collapsed once more, sobbing from the agony.

"Stop! Please!" I cried, my body convulsing and seizing from the torturous pain as I dragged that leg, now limp, behind me.

A giggle rang out. "I thought I was yours to play with? Are you tired of playing, Zeke?" I felt her breath right in front of me, but I was too afraid to open my eyes and face what I'd see, what she might do to me if my eyes were open.

I clenched my eyelids shut, my nose dripping snot as I trembled weakly, waiting for the heat of her breath to dissipate.

I heard the crunch of a leaf and a cackle in the distance.

"Seven," Harkins announced.

"Eight!" She didn't wait, shouting happily from somewhere in front of me.

I moaned in pain, whimpering as the cold of the night began to settle into my bones—I must have been losing blood quickly. Dropping my chest to the ground in exhaustion, I dragged myself through the hay, army crawling an inch or two before the blinding ache forced me to give up.

"Nine," Harkins' voice came from right behind me.

"Oh fuck, shit, please, Jesus," I breathed out, panic coursing through every vein in my body as I spiraled in the dark, unsure which left I had taken and which right would come next. I dropped down to the ground, sobbing from the pain and from the panic, when I felt a large hand grip me by my hair.

I yelled, snarling as Harkins yanked me by my hair, forcing me to look at the black leather boots in front of me.

"Ten," she whispered, standing tall above me in all her terrifying power. "I think we hurt him too much. He barely moved." She shrugged her disappointment while twirling that damn knife in her hand.

Harkins remained silent, his only contribution how hard he gripped at my short hair, threatening to rip the strands from my scalp.

"Okay, okay, okay, okay." She paced maniacally before coming to a halt again. "Okay!" She smiled so large, the corners of her mouth stretched from ear to ear, almost inhuman in this light. "I have an idea! What if we just let you go, and you don't tell anyone? What do you think?" she said all sweetly, batting her eyelids at me as if I had any say anymore.

Snot dripped down to my lip, my body turning unbearably cold as my fingertips went numb. I mustered a nod, wrapping my arms around myself for comfort.

"Fine," Camila said with a bored tone to her voice. "Go then." She waved her hand in the air like she was tired of me.

I wasted no second of that opportunity. The minute Harkins' hand softened on my head, I crawled through the hay, ignoring every burn, every itch, every agonizing pain in my torn flesh as I slid my body through the corridors, hauling myself forward with my heart thundering in my chest.

I was going to get out of here.

That crazy bitch was going to let me out of here.

The tears fell down my cheeks freely as I took my next left turn, only to find her there, waiting for me with that sick, twisted smile painted over her face. My heart sank deep into my stomach, watching as she twirled the end of one of her braids with her finger. A giggle began to bubble out from her chest, growing into a full-on cackle as she tossed her head back in amusement. Bile rose up in my throat as I collapsed to the ground on my back.

This was it.

NINE
BLOOD PLAY

"Look at him; he's so pathetic." I sneered, all association of him being a person, having a life, feelings, or a future completely erased from my mind.

All I could see him for was someone who was going to cost me my future.

He was blubbering now, disgusting and weak, the way men always became when they realized they weren't the ones with all the power. He was nothing to me, only someone who was a risk to my future, a risk to Harkins' career.

I would have fucked him had he just asked, but now, I was going to take everything from him. I looked back at Harkins.

Somewhere in the dark of the maze, my rage had grown, and every Kappa piece of shit who walked past me, throwing an underhanded comment about the performance Noah gave them the previous night, added to my anger.

I couldn't handle it anymore. I wasn't going to be someone who was laughed at, an inside joke between all of them. Noah was the first to go. I found him separated from his group of friends, getting a blowjob from Delaney Summers. It was easy to slit her throat— he barely noticed when the slurping turned to gurgling and I pulled her off his cock for a humble death.

That's when I stabbed him through the balls, slicing them open before he dropped to his knees, the look on his face, the realization when he'd seen it was me who was ending his life, fucking delectable. I licked his blood from my fingers before I continued on to the maze, one after another, cutting down any of his little friends and their crew of loyal whores I came across.

Kyle Danvers needed to spend the rest of his life giving thanks to whatever God who made it so that my best friend saved his ass. I would have loved to see what he looked like on the sharp end of my knife. Lucky for him, he stuck by her, and they made it out of the maze. I looked back at Harkins, standing there, feeling nothing but reassurance as he waited for me, supporting me to do what I needed to get through this.

This man saw me at my darkest and worst, at my most vile and vulnerable. Instead of asking how he could save me, he asked if I needed saving at all.

I didn't, but I did want him there for it.

I stood over Ezekiel, one foot on the outside of each hip as I dropped down to sit on his waist. My knife came down sloppily, stabbing him in the bicep as I caught myself from falling forward onto him. He cried from the pain, coughing and screaming as he continued to beg for help, beg for me to come to my senses, beg Harkins to release him.

"Can you feel how wet I still am?" I asked, grinding my hips over his exposed stomach, a trail of my arousal painted down his skin. "Everytime you scream, I just want to fuck it out of you more."

His head moved from side to side, a groan of anguish all he could muster as I ripped open his jeans and pulled his cock from his pants. "Can you get hard while you're in pain?" I asked, pulling the knife from his arm and forcing another pained screech from his lungs. "Do you think he'll come before he dies?" I asked my professor, who looked down at me in admiration.

He bit his lip, looking me up and down, covered in blood and bathed in moonlight. "Let's test it out," he said, grabbing at the hardened bulge straining his pants. I wanted to feel his cock inside me. I was aching to feel it stretch me wide, but I knew he wouldn't fit.

Not yet.

I squeezed the base of Ezekiel's cock, feeling it harden again under my tight hold as I undid the buttons of my mesh top with my free hand. I pulled my breasts out from the black tube top bra, but before I had a chance to rub my hand over the pert flesh,

I felt Harkins behind me. His hand was large, ungloved, hot, and rough against the soft skin of my breasts, his fingers tugging at my nipples as I ground back and forth against Zeke's cock, slowly bringing it to life against his will as he sobbed in agony beneath me.

"Is this not what you wanted?" I said breathily, each jerk of my hips sparking pleasure through my center as I used him for my own needs, rubbing my cunt up and down until the need to come began to build inside me again.

"Please," he begged, but my only response was a cry of bliss from the feel of Demetri's fingers pushing through my folds, rubbing delicately over each nerve ending until I felt like I was going to burst.

I felt his fingers sliding inside of me, coaxing desperate mewls from my lips as he rubbed against the walls of my pussy, finding the spot that had me biting the inside of my cheek studs and going blind to my surroundings.

"Please!" Zeke shouted through pained sobs.

"Please," I moaned, begging Demetri for more as I tilted my hips back to him, begging for him to fill me in whatever way he wanted.

Instead, it was the head of Zeke's cock I felt against my pussy, molten hot and dripping in anticipation. My professor's hands guided our prey deep inside of me as I sobbed, my body on fire, sensitive to every feeling and needy for release.

"Oh fuck," I whispered, feeling the full sensation of Ezekiel's length bottoming out inside of me.

I shifted back onto Zeke's lap, my hands on his chest as I rode his cock. Demetri's left hand guided my hip in slow rolls while the other stretched me further open, his fingers spearing inside of me, readying my cunt for him.

"He looks like he's fading." Harkins noted as Zeke's eyes dimmed, closing in slow, lazy blinks as his mouth parted. His fingers moving in unison with Ezekiel's cock between my legs, splitting me open.

"Don't you want to come before you die?" I smacked his face, bringing him back to the present, a cold laugh rising from my throat.

He groaned, his teeth chattering despite his cock remaining rock hard and hot inside of me.

I dragged the knife down his chest, slicing far enough for a line of blood to follow behind the blade and drip down his side.

"Oops, too deep," I laughed, Harkins pulling my hips down as he moved, filling my ass with three slick fingers.

"Fuck," I groaned, throwing my head back and biting my lip.

He moved them in and out skillfully, rubbing along the wall that was stretched by Ezekiel's cock inside me. I shuddered, gasping from pleasure as he drove me closer to the brink of oblivion.

I was almost there. I felt maddened by the need to come, to unravel and break apart as I stole from someone who wanted to take from me.

"More," I begged Demetri, my moans becoming louder with each bounce of my hips against Zeke's erection.

His eyes fluttered beneath me, like there was nothing left for him to cling to except the hope to go peacefully.

How boring.

"He's dying," I told the professor, slowing my hips to match the rhythm of his fingers in my ass. "He's still so hard, though." I groaned, squeezing my breasts, leaving bloody handprints over my nipples as I reached down to drag my knife across his chest again.

Every slice forced his eyes open, just for another second while he convulsed and twitched from the pain. It was addicting, the way his cock jerked inside of me every time he got closer to death, the way it swelled and begged for release even though the pain was far too great for him to come.

I looked back to see Demetri rubbing himself through his pants with his free hand, his other still working my ass. "Fuck me, please," I whispered to him, licking my lips once he pulled his cock free from his pants.

It looked bigger than the last time.

Impossibly big.

He leaned over me anyway, ready to finally fill me up like he'd promised.

Two fingers stretched my cunt, squeezing in with Ezekiel's cock while three fingers continued to play inside my ass. I begged, cried, prayed to a God I didn't believe in while my professor stuck a third, and then a fourth, finger into my pussy.

"More!" I was desperate for my release, my nails stabbing into Ezekiel's flesh, blood pebbling where they sank deep.

I gasped, my head spinning each time Demetri's fingers moved in perfect rhythm against Zeke's cock. How could so much fit inside of me? I knew it was nothing compared to what he would feel like. I was so full, burning with pleasure, yet somehow still aching for more.

As long as it came from him.

"I need more lube," he hummed in my ear.

The sloppy sounds of his fingers sliding in and out made me think I was wet enough for whatever he'd need, but I didn't argue. A guttural sound left me as he spread me open, pushing a final finger inside me. There was a burn, a sting of discomfort with his thumb added, proving him right. The pain was a mark in my soul, a proof of ownership, that he was making me his, adjusting my body to his needs so I could take him the way he deserved to be taken.

Worshiped.

Fully.

I lifted my knife in the air, stabbing down directly below Zeke's sternum, a gurgling, pained sound coming from his throat as the knife tore its way down his stomach. He convulsed as I rode his cock with Demetri's hand inside me, both of us trembling as I came and he took his final, sputtered breaths.

Demetri slowed, his hand still moving, uncaring that I had already climaxed. Before I'd gotten a chance to come down from the high of the orgasm, he moved his wrist in and out of me. Nothing but incoherent gargles making their way from my mouth, I was so far gone to the mixture of pleasure and pain.

Every movement was overload on my senses. My pussy quaking around his wrist, with the smallest jerk or twitch.

One finger at a time, he slowly pulled his way out of me, until I felt nearly hollow, aside from the dead man's dick I was still skewered onto.

I reached my fingers into the split skin, my nails digging into the parted flesh, tearing into the muscle until I could feel his insides under my fingers.

"It's so warm," I said breathily, throwing my head back as I let my hands explore inside the dead boy's stomach.

Lifting my hands out of him, I turned to face my professor, Ezekiel's dick falling out of me as I took two bloody hands and coated Demetri's cock with them, rubbing in portions of what was likely Zeke's guts and using them as lubricant. He moaned, relishing in the feel of the warm blood drenching his cock.

He removed his cloak, placing it on the ground next to me like a blanket.

"More?" I asked, draping my voice in a sticky, sweet accent.

"Yeah," he breathed out, both of us groaning at the sound of my hands squelching through Zeke's stomach.

I held up a handful of blood, fisting his cock as I covered every inch of him in it. He gently pushed me down to the cloak, my back on the ground as he hovered over me, his hand cupping my cheek.

He was trembling, but so was I.

I felt the head of his cock, hot and wet, pressing at my entrance, his fingers guiding the swollen head in. It already felt like too much, too thick to possibly fit inside, but my body craved him anyway, my hips undulating in response to his proximity.

"Please," I begged, my voice a ghost of a whisper caught in the wind.

With a grunt, he pushed the head of his cock all the way, making an almost popping sound once it made it through. I squirmed away desperately, already too full from just the tip. I was going to split in half from the rest, no doubt.

"Oh fuck, oh fuck," I breathed out in panic, his arm hooked under my back to keep me from inching away.

"You wanted this, Camila," he reminded me, like he himself needed me to confirm it.

I nodded, licking my lips as I shifted again, feeling the head of his cock everywhere inside me all at once.

Was it bigger than his hand?

I groaned. "You're too big, it's too much," I gasped, my words struggling to come as my eyes welled with tears.

It was overwhelming to be so full.

"You can take it, baby. I know you can." I felt his hand caressing the side of my cheek, a surge of warmth fluttering in my chest from the encouragement.

I nodded back, feeling him pull out just slightly before thrusting an inch deeper.

"Oh God. Fuck." I clawed my hands down his chest, my hips moving desperately again as the feeling of fullness began to give me pleasure on top of the pain.

"Yeah, just like that," he breathed out, his fingers making music over my clit in precise movements.

I dropped my head back, writhing in pure, magical bliss as he filled me up, inch by inch. "I wish you could see how pretty you look, your cunt stretched open for me like this." I propped myself on my elbows to see him, his fat cock buried deep inside my pussy. It felt like an entire minute went by before he moved again, and I was dripping with need, ready to take whatever he would give.

"Shit," I hissed, the pressure already immense, my body aching to give out again, to explode with another orgasm.

He pulled back slowly, his left hand still tracing circles on my clit when he thrusted back in, sheathing himself once more inside of me. "Demetri," I breathed out, my hands grasping for any part of him I could reach.

"Wrap your legs around me," he instructed, lifting me off the ground.

The minute he shifted my hips up, my body became a live wire, sensitive to every heightened feeling in my overstimulated body. I felt like I couldn't hear anything anymore; sounds were dull but sharp, smells blended, my vision grayed.

"Look at you, milking my cock so greedily." His hand brushed against my forehead, moving sticky, wet strands of hair out of the way. "Are you with me?" His gravelly voice pulled me from the subspace, and I clung to him as he moved us, never once releasing my legs.

I nodded as I leaned forward, pressing my lips to his as my heart filled with heat.

"Good," he chuckled. "You aren't done yet." His canines were white in the moonlight, his smirk somewhat menacing. "He's still hard."

I realized he was talking about Zeke, and that when he moved us, it was to put me back on top of his corpse. Demetri's hand reached past me, squelching around inside the cavity I'd made in Zeke's stomach. His hand stroked up and down beneath me, slathering blood on Ezekiel's still-alive cock.

"Ready?" he asked, waiting for my nod of approval before using the dead man beneath us as a sex toy.

He started slowly at first, until the head had fully pushed past the tight ring of my ass.

I gasped noisily, shaking my head. "It's too much!" I protested, but his mouth found mine.

I melted at the soft warmth of his lips distracting me as he continued to stuff me full with another man's cock.

He stilled inside of me, a low growl vibrating in his chest as he stared into my eyes. "You're the most beautiful thing I've ever seen, and I've been waiting for too long to tell you that."

A tear fell from the corner of my eye, dropping down my temple. He didn't wait for me to respond, pulling halfway out and thrusting back into me, urgent grunts escaping his throat as he got closer to the edge.

"Say you're mine," he whispered, a desperate sound coming from his throat as he used my pussy for his pleasure. "Say you're my dirty little whore, using a dead man's cock to make you come."

"I'm yours. I'm yours," I offered back, my voice breathy, shaky, like this promise would mean so much more than just tonight.

He moved in and out of me, setting me on fire from the inside out, my pussy drenched, a dripping mess stretched over his fat, veiny cock. His mouth pressed to me again, his tongue dancing with mine as he held me tight, my body seizing in one, final orgasm. I felt his hand press over my mouth to muffle out my screaming, my cum gushing out of me in a force so powerful, it pushed him out of me along with Zeke.

He chuckled, fisting himself a few more times, his cock coated in my cum, entering me only halfway before he spilled his release inside of me.

"Fuck," he breathed out, his cock jerking in and out of me still, like it had a mind of its own.

I laughed, unable to do anything else with my spent body as he wrapped his arms around me and rolled us back over to his cloak on the ground. It wasn't much, but this hay was unbearable, and anything would prove to help protect against it.

Demetri pulled me into his side, where I draped one leg over his, and we stayed frozen for a moment in time, staring at the stars.

"I just fucked my professor," I whispered, like I was telling him the biggest secret of my life.

His response was a crooked smile, but he didn't turn his face to look at me yet.

"Don't think this means you don't owe me that thesis." His voice was deep and authoritative, but I could hear the playfulness behind it.

He finger-walked his hand down my belly and across my hips before sliding down between my legs again, the shreds of my panties provided no barrier as he scooped his cum dripping out of me and pushed it back inside. My breath hitched, my thighs squeezing together as if to help.

I smiled the biggest most genuine smile I'd probably let out in three years. Dropping my ear to his chest, I let the soothing melody of his heartbeat calm me down. It felt like an hour, though probably only a few minutes had passed, when all the blood and cum began to dry over my skin and itch like a fucking nightmare.

Dark haired girls were normally blessed with extra body hair, and I wasn't going to be able to just pick or rub this shit off of me unless I was going for a wax-job.

"I guess all good things must end." He let out a sad smile, coming to a stand before extending his hand to help me up.

We brushed the loose hay off, knowing it was the only thing we really had control over now.

It was time to face the music.

Time to go back to reality.

TEN
THE END

"What are you doing?" I watched from a few feet behind as he took a lighter from his pocket and held the flame up against Ezekiel's clothing.

"Fixing this," he said with little inflection, as if there was a part of him that had been activated to take care of moments like these.

Like this was something he was good at.

He moved around the corpse, letting the flame touch everywhere it could so the fire could build as fast as possible. Within seconds, Ezekiel's entire body was up in flames, the smoke becoming too heady for us to stay in that segment of the maze.

"We need to get the fuck out of here, *now*," Harkins commanded, his tone of authority much like the one he used in his class. It always did something to me.

Even more so now that I knew what he felt like inside of me.

He grabbed me by the hand, fingers wrapping tightly between mine as he pulled me through the maze. There was no confusion in the way he moved, knowing which turns to take and which ones to avoid. I'd recognized so many of the landmarks from when I wandered the maze, lost and desperately hoping for a way out.

That's when I realized how clean the maze was, how he had pulled the bodies out of sight, deep into the corn. For me.

To protect me.

We slowed down, reaching what seemed to be the end. I squeezed his hand, and he returned it with a squeeze of his own, finally looking down at me.

"You're perfect," he whispered, brushing a strand of hair behind my ear with his free hand.

We both looked down to where our fingers tangled together, like they weren't ready to accept their fate. Out there, we couldn't exist. Not yet. I swallowed a hard lump, wishing the tears back into my eyes and praying they wouldn't fall and embarrass me.

How cringe could I possibly be? Crying over a hook-up.

Naya would never let me live it down.

He gave me one more squeeze, our fingers parting slowly, my heart breaking all at once. What would we be after this?

Had we ever been anything at all?

We took slow steps, side by side, until we made our final turn, the exit of the maze directly in front of us. It was blinding, an array of lights that were shocking to the senses after being trapped in the darkness of that maze for so long. Flashlights and spotlights dropped onto us, forcing me to shield my eyes from the brightness.

I could hear a drone of people speaking, calling out for help, and then dozens of men in uniforms suddenly appeared.

"I got her here," Harkins called out, "I got her." He put his hands over my shoulders like he was holding on to me, keeping me from moving.

Trapping me in place.

The cops rushed to us, my heart sinking deep into my stomach, a heavy boulder of hot magma in my guts. Bile rose to my throat, but I wasn't sure I could swallow it down. He was going to turn me in. After all of that, Harkins was going to turn me in.

Had all of it been an act? The brilliance of a man who knew what to do to keep himself alive?

I dropped to my knees, vomit spewing from my throat in a bitter wave. My arms shook as they held me up, and I couldn't hear what was being said above me, my heart hammering too loudly. I didn't have the strength to lift my head and face my betrayer.

I heaved once more, the final contents of my stomach spewing onto the dying grass and an unfortunate pig's leather shoes. "There's no more students in there?" I heard from above.

"No, she was the last one." Harkins voice sounded clearer again.

I wiped my mouth, taking deep breaths as I felt the pressure of his fingertips against my shoulder.

"She's covered in blood; did he hurt her?" a female voice asks.

"I don't think so. I found them just in time. She was fighting back and together, we were able to stop him." He was painting an entirely new story, convincing them that Ezekiel was the killer, the two of us his lucky victims who escaped.

"Let's get you checked out in the back of the EMT van." The woman knelt in front of me, placing her hand on my shoulder.

I shook my head. "I want to go home. I don't want to be touched by anyone."

"I'll let them know," she agreed, seeing the state I was in as proof that enough trauma had happened.

"Hey, that's my best friend!" I heard her voice in the distance like barbed wire around a chicken's neck. "Mila!" Naya cried out, pushing grown men out of the way as she fell to her knees in front of me.

"I thought you were dead! You stopped answering the phone!" she blubbered, crying as she showed me how many times she had tried calling me. "They wouldn't let me go back in there. I would have gone back for you, bitch, I promise!" she sobbed, the guilt tearing her apart.

I'd never tell her, of course, not this one. This secret belonged to me and Demetri only. She pulled me into her arms, and I let her, reassuring her I was okay, and that, most importantly, there was nothing I held against her.

"Is that smoke?" another cop asked from the other side.

They began to scatter, more popping out of the woodwork now that the problem was something they couldn't solve with their guns. Funny how they were all too scared to get lost inside a maze with a killer, though.

I disguised my amusement as concern for the corn.

"Oh shit, the corn maze is on fire. Call for a firetruck, now!" an angry, masculine voice sounded above me.

"I don't know boss, sounds like a good way to clean this shit up, keep the town from panicking over a dead serial killer," the female cop said, still knelt down to my level.

I bit back a smile.

Fucking Ohio.

EPILOGUE

"Are you sure I need all three of these Monstera plants?" he asked, a smirk pulling at the corner of his lip, putting those dimples in full display.

"You're fucking with me, I know it." I shook my head, handing him another oversized plant pot.

We were decorating his office with some of the leftover plants we didn't have space for at home, now that I was turning in the keys to my dorm. Naya was a lot of things, but I was thankful she was tolerant of the fact that I'd turned our dorm room into a jungle over the last four years at NPC. So, here we were, bringing a few extras to his office to brighten it up for next semester.

He faked being too weak, dropping to the ground on his back with my plant still in his arms.

"Be careful! That's my Adansonii Albo. She paid for my bachelors," I laughed, taking my prized possession from his arms and finding a spot for it in front of the window.

"Are you happy now? I'll have your plants to keep me company every day." He grinned, smelling the leaf like it was a fucking flower or something. "Let's go unload that moving truck." He nodded out the window, where the truck waited for us.

I wasn't going very far. NPC was a big campus, and now that I'd graduated, I had to move out of the dorms. Thanks to Demetri, I'd be moving into faculty housing. Lucky for us, there were no rules about faculty dating, so when he got me the job in the botany department and we applied for the same house on campus, no one even batted an eye.

Either they thought we were sharing rent, or they simply didn't give a fuck.

"Yes," I admitted, finding that with him, it was easier to be happy. I draped my arms over his neck and he dropped his head down, pressing his forehead to mine.

"Something on your mind, gorgeous?" he asked, like he already had the power to see through my smiles when something was rotting in my brain.

"What if I'm not a good teacher?" I whispered, letting my insecurities show.

He barked out a loud laugh, lifting my chin so my gaze could meet his. "Then I'll pay you to be my gardener."

I pushed him off, playing like I was upset at the joke.

"You know I'm kidding, beautiful. The school is always looking for a groundskeeper." He laughed again, too loud and infectious for me to keep up the farce.

I cracked a smile, giving him my middle finger as I slowly stepped back from him. He knew where my fears were rooted; just because you were good at something, like keeping plants alive, didn't mean you were qualified to teach others.

I was hoping I was, but I knew what Demetri was getting at with his jokes. *It wouldn't be the end of the world if I wasn't.*

"Are you threatening a professor, Miss Machado?" he said in his sternest voice.

I couldn't hold the laugh in. "With my middle finger, *professor*?" I played his game, knowing that if I pushed, I would get the result I wanted.

We'd kept our relationship secret until I finished my degree. I worked my ass off to make sure I met my early graduation deadline at the end of fall semester, so we only had a few weeks of hiding. A month or so of him sneaking into my dorm at night through the window, pretending to be a student dropping in for a hook-up, a few torturous weeks of me looking down at my desk for the entirety of his labs because I knew I'd give something away if I caught even a glimpse of his gorgeous face.

Still, the weeks did eventually pass, and despite Naya nearly dying from holding onto the secret as if it was a tampon threatening to give her toxic shock syndrome, we all made it through.

I was no longer a student.

I was an employee at our university.

We could be together.

This man, who knew me exactly for who I was, had seen my darkest parts as well as my light and thought both were equally beautiful. This man, who I never once thought would belong to me, because what would ever make me so lucky?

I guess the lucky part was being dumped by Noah.

I'd still be the quarterback's girlfriend if it wasn't for him, and what a boring Halloween that would have been.

He circled the desk after me, hands grazing the wood as he fought to keep me in his little trap. I couldn't move a step in any direction but forward without him catching me.

I ran towards the wall, but he grabbed me by the waist, pressing my back to his front as my legs wiggled. I laughed, a hearty one born from the center of my chest. It was the sound of true happiness, and it had felt so foreign for so long. With Noah, everything was dull, gray. I'd stopped questioning whether it was love or whether it was what I deserved, because I thought, 'at least I'm not alone.'

No, settling for someone who barely tolerated me was the worst thing I had done to myself. Numbed my senses just before I'd stepped out into a lightning storm, as if it somehow would protect me.

Every day with Demetri was a day I felt loved to the fullest capacity, accepted, worshiped.

"What if Noah had never broken up with me?" I whispered, almost afraid to ask as I turned my head back to look at him, his arms still holding me tightly.

He brought me down to the ground, spinning me to face him as he pinned me against his desk. "Look at me, Camila." I obeyed, my eyes shifting from the ground to focus on the hard lines between his eyebrows. "Noah What's-his-face was a fucking idiot for leaving you, but it was the smartest thing he ever did." I quirked an eyebrow up. "It was torture seeing him with you. In my head, I'd already killed him a million ways, but I knew that if I killed him for real, you'd never love me. Not if I took him from you. Not if I broke your heart."

His confession was too honest, too raw, too vulnerable for it to have been meant for someone as wretched and vile as me, but he liked to remind me that he wasn't so innocent either. That's what these confessions were about. I smiled, lifting up onto the table and spreading my legs open to give him the space to step between them.

His hands came down on my bare thighs with a hard slap, and I hissed, throwing my head back as his mouth found my neck. Soft kisses made their way up my jaw line as skilled fingers worked to spread my legs open, no underwear to be found under my skirt.

He shifted his gaze back up to my face, and I bit my lip. Discreet was never enough for him. I knew it, too. It just made him demand that I ask for it even more. "Why aren't you wearing panties?" he growled.

Still chewing on my bottom lip, I finally gave it a rest to answer his question. "I was hoping I'd trip and maybe fall on a dildo or two on the way here." A scream left my throat from the force of him flipping me and bending me over the table. As he lifted my skirt up to expose my ass completely, a cold wind brushed against my flesh, pebbling it as he readied me for what would come next.

I moaned in anticipation, and he coughed out a laugh, trying not to break character in this little game. His palm came down hard, the sharp sting burning over my ass. I'd yelled, I was sure of it, but before I could cry from the pain, his hand was there, rubbing softly over the angry skin.

Again, another slap, his hand coming down harder this time, with less reservation and more delay before he began to soothe me. I groaned, my hips thrusting into the air as my body begged for what it really wanted, what it really needed.

"Already, Camila? Look at you, dripping for my cock to stretch you open, ruin you for anyone else." Two fingers slipped inside of me, a gasp falling from my lips as I felt how truly wet I was.

"Please, Demetri," I begged, my voice a quiet whisper as I looked back at him.

Those green eyes were everything.

Three fingers found their way inside me, moving in and out as they rubbed against my g-spot while his thumb stayed pressed to my clit. I sobbed, my mouth already watering at the thought of the fourth finger coming next.

It never disappointed, stretching me open and getting me ready for him. The light sting was nothing in comparison to the initial burn of his cock in moments like these, where we couldn't spend all day slowly working up to it.

He reached over me, opening his top drawer and pulling out a bottle of lube. My paranoia from my ex's infidelity would have made me suspicious if we hadn't already fucked in his office three times this week. At this point, I just considered him well prepared. He kept his hand on my back, pressing me down so that my chest was flat against his desk, all four fingers moving steadily in and out of me.

I heard his zipper, then the lube being squeezed from the bottle, unable to see much from my angle except the way that Death Star tattoo made his arm somehow look more defined and muscular.

Saliva dripped from my open lips onto his desk as we both savored the initial feeling of the head of his cock entering me,—how tight my cunt hugged his erection, how his swollen cock struggled to fit inside me.

It reminded me that I was his. Every time I felt the inexplicable burn of my pussy being abused by his cock, it reminded me that if I weren't made for him, I wouldn't be able to take it. I wouldn't be able to let him fuck me and split me open and then put me back together so that I'd be limping when I left this office.

After a few moments of adjusting, he pulled back, drenching himself in more lubricant before thrusting in what I assumed to be halfway. Halfway stuffed, because I wasn't yet overwhelmed.

Halfway because I was still greedy for more.

I pushed my hips back onto him, my silent plea to keep going.

He chuckled, a hand working its way around me, fingers slipping between my thighs to rub my most sensitive parts. I shuddered, thighs clenching together on instinct as he thrusted even deeper.

"You want me to stuff you full of my cum?" he asked, his voice laced in that husky confidence.

"Yes. Please," I begged, reaching back for his hip, trying to force him deeper inside me.

He knocked my hand out of the way, grabbing both my wrists and pinning them to my back with a single, large hand. With the other, he came down on my ass once more, the noise sounding nearly inhuman as it made its way out of my mouth. Every part of me was needy for release, aching to be well fucked.

He pulled back, this time pushing his hips forward slowly, teasing my body and my mind as he stretched me open. It drove me mad; I was sopping wet and desperate to be railed until my brain chemistry changed, and here he was, savoring it, moving lazily. I felt like one more thrust would blow me over the edge. I'd erupt and cum my brains out all over his desk.

He grabbed my hair, twisting it around his wrist before sinking deep inside me until I was left slack jaw-ed and wet-eyed at the feeling of his balls pressing against me. He tugged at my hair, pulling my head up and whispering into my ear. "Tell me how you want it, baby."

"Hard, *professor*," I gritted out, bracing myself for what would come next.

While still pinning me to the desk with one hand, he used the other to grip my hip, holding me steady as he fucked me faster and harder than ever before. "Fuck," I cried, my cheek wet from the pile of drool gathered under my face as my pussy seized and quaked through my orgasm.

"I'll never get tired of seeing your pretty little cunt stretch for me," he said, gently releasing my wrists and bringing both hands to my hips. "Hold on," he warned, a dark chuckle leaving his mouth.

Reaching forward, I stretched my arms straight out in front of me, gripping the edge of his desk while he fucked me within an inch of my life. My body shook, the orgasm not quite ending as each stroke pushed against my g-spot, continuing the sensation until all I felt was an uncomfortable need to explode.

I ripped open like a waterfall, tearing all around me with beautiful violence as I let go, drenching his cock with my cum. One final thrust was all he needed before he was following me, spilling inside of me as he pulled me even closer. My back was flush against his chest now, his cock still pulsing while his hands gripped me tight. "I love you," he whispered in my ear.

"I love you," I returned with a smile, melting into his hold.

I guess Ohio would do.

As long as I got to do it with him.

Books by Santana:

Standalone:

Heartless Heathens: A why-choose, Gothic Romance

Reina del Cártel Series: (complete)

Queen of Nothing (Book 1)

Reign of Ruin (Book 2)

Empire of Carnage (Book 3)

Diablos Locos Motorcycle Club:

No Place for Devils (book 1)

No Mercy for the Depraved (book 2)

Novellas:

Dreams of truth: A Dark Romantasy novella

No Way Out: A Halloween Erotic Horror

About the author

Santana Knox is the pen name of a Brazilian writer, neuro-divergent creative, follower of Santa Muerte and self acclaimed Witch who emerges from the foulest swamp bogs to bring you even filthier stories. Santana got tired of letting the voices in her head drive her crazy, and decided to write down the stories they were begging to tell instead. A lover of the unusual, and a hopeless romantic when it comes to toxic villains, Santana's books should always be taken with a grain of salt, specifically the kind that keeps demons away.

Join Santana's cult (Reading group) for bonus content, early looks, and sneak previews: Santana Knox's Heathens on facebook.

Instagram: @Santana.knox